THE POWER OF ZERO

ZERO

AND OTHER SCI-FI STORIES

MR ANANT

To Readers

who think like me

Contents

PREFACE

If no other intelligence deserves to be called scientific but that which comprises the purview of our comprehension or aids in enlarging our material possessions, then science fiction based on the ancient Vedic mythology has no claim to the concept. But if that intelligence which takes us beyond the limited world and our pea-sized brains, gives us fresh energy, makes us creative, and happy can be part of science, then we profess the appelation to the concept. For the Vedic mythology lends itself to science fiction seamlessly; and science fiction opens up minds to myriad possibilities, some more real thanothers. Without a knowledge of Vedic mythology so rich in technological concepts masqueraded as magic or mystery, much of the elegance' in Indian science fiction cannot be appreciated nor understood. When *Vishwakarma* , the architect deity builds the *Pushpaka Vimana*, an aircraft, or *Droupadi* in Mahabharata uses the inexhaustible vessel, *Akshyapatra*, the concepts are not in the realm of mysterious powers of magic but the harnessing of the power of technology, but which are lost to the readers, ignorant of the power of logical deductions. As a matter of fact, Vedic epics and stories abounds in scinece and technology. The short stories in the science fiction collection is an attempt to blend in the modern technology with the magical notions in Vedic times.

Acknowledgements

Special thanks goes to one and only person: my spouse, who believes that I have a great potential as a writer.

Prologue

Any object is either present or absent. Duality is prevalent in everything as opposites: air and space; sound and silence; and everything and nothing, or so it seems. However, in reality, the earth so full of objects and surrounded by air hangs in invisible space; sounds discernible to the human ear are part of a spectrum of inaudible frequencies otherwise known as silence. The all-inclusive nothingness reigns supreme, and the key to which lies in the human heart; therefore, unlocking it evolves the mind.

I

108 Circumambulations

"You gotta be kidding me," said CEO Elon Bezo, springing to his feet and walking away only to stop midway. He arched his face slowly; there was a slight frown. Continuing, "From what I know, you are Indians requesting a discount on space tickets. Well, although we are open to customization, would you mind telling me the purpose of your —err— venture?" he asked.

"Sure," replied a tall, dark-skinned man, forehead smeared with sacred ash, looking over his shoulders at the rest of his team and bobbing his head towards them. Tightening the saffron belt-like cloth over a glaring yellow shirt, he continued unperturbed, "Your space ticket – return ticket – includes training, launch support services, air and life support, and medical services. But we need a one-way ticket, not a return ticket. We would also like you to remove the support services of air and medical."

Bezo rolled his eyes. Bending over and leaning his hands on the table, he looked up to face the team of six. Bezo opened his mouth to utter something, but before that, the leader of the team, Thalaivar began an explanation.

"We belong to the Kavadi community. Our forefathers had been practicing the holy dance, *Kavadiyattam* for centuries. This is for a sacred mission that started during the Tamil *Sangam* period – the third century C.E. It may appear unscientific to you, even insensible. But, I request you to hear me out with patience."

"Okay." Bezo shrugged. He sat down.

"To put it in simple words: we have been circumambulating mother earth."

"Sorry?" Bezo leaned forward.

Thalaivar continued in a nonchalant voice. "Our god – the six-faced Lord Muruga – flew around the world thrice on his revered peacock vehicle while competing with his brother for a prize – a knowledge-laden ripe mango – from their parents: Lord Shiva and Goddess Parvathi. As he didn't win, we, his devotees, have been continuing the circling with a missionary zeal."

Bezo stared at him blankly. Then, he blinked.

"Yeah, we get that a lot." Thalaivar gave a benign smile.

There was a brief pause.

"And, just how did you go around the world all these centuries?" Bezo asked in a casual tone.

"There have been many ways: walks, boats, and planes adapting our mission to the trending technology over centuries."

"How many have you completed? That is, if you have had a count of it," Bezo said, curling his lips.

"107. We are on our last one, the hundred and eighth, now with a used submarine."

Bezo raised his eyebrows. Another pause ensued. After a while, he scrunched his eyes and shook his head quickly.

"So, how is this space trip related to your circumambulations?"

"We want to complete our final circumambulation and offer our prayers to Lord Muruga in space," Thalaivar said, the trademark imperturbable tone continuing..

Bezo relaxed and took a deep breath. "Your purpose is reasonable alright. But what exactly is the motivation for a one-way trip?"

Thalaivar pursed his lips for a second, and Bezo wondered if he had offended the sect in any way. "You see, this is unusual. It is the first time a customer is requesting a one-way, in fact." Bezo explained.

Continuing an undisturbed composure, Thalaivar said, "It's our belief that we should not return in the same vehicle. Call it culture, customs or practices. But, don't worry, after a while, the Indian spaceship will arrive in that direction. We've made arrangements to hop onto it."

"I see. So, I suppose you have supplies for the 'while' in space."

"Exactly. We've come to an agreement with ISRO, the Indian Space Research Organisation to provide supplies. It starts after six months—the time we will be taking for our last circumambulation."

"Six? Surely, you can do it in three. I've heard that it could take as little as forty days."

"Well, we make a few stops at the lord's temples on our way."

"Of course. Of course" Bezo nodded hastily in agreement. After a moment, he said, "We will need to see the agreement you have with ISRO. After all, we are responsible for the safety of our customers."

"No problem. There is another thing. I think it may not be quite difficult for your spaceship to drop us. Astronauts perform spacewalks, don't they? In this case, however, it would be space pray, I believe."

"Spacewalks are dangerous. Even for trained astronauts, they are physically demanding. Such long spacewalks have never been attempted so to speak," Bezo's face turned grave,

"Not to worry. Adequate supplies will keep us going."

Bezo did not seem convinced.

"ISRO has promised to send an emergency spaceship," Thalaivar said.

"And about the year-long training?"

"For centuries, we've had a rigorous and spartan lifestyle. For the *Kavadi* dance, we follow painful rituals of body-piercing and fire-walking. Luckily, it will be simple for us to adapt to the space venture training. What would take several months of training can be done in the next six months " Thalaivar clicked his Apple iPad to demonstrate a video where one such ritual was performed by his team.

The sounds at the Vandenberg Space Force Base became fainter as Bezo's mind floated to the southern coastal tip of India. Far from the man-made worlds that he lived in, the whiff of a bygone era crept into his consciousness. High on a hill, nestled in thick, green forests, the angry little son of Shiva stood in the temple at Palani, slighted at being tricked by his elder brother. He literally went around the world thrice, and his fat, lazy brother went about eating all the while. When Muruga was on his last trip, the clever brother simply went around his parents. Yet, he won. These Kavadis had been patiently at work, century after century, going round and round in circles. Could mankind take up such meaningless missions? Could the purpose based on folklores be any less foolish? Drifting back, Bezo sat upright. He should not allow such thoughts to permeate his mind: customer is king.

"Agreed. We'll take a few tests before and after the training," replied Bezo, "But I'm worried about your spending time in space. Although you may carry adequate oxygen supply, there are other issues. It's extremely cold out there – you'd freeze in -120 degrees. Then, the sun burns you, and that is, +120 degrees. And, then, there's nasty radiation from the rest of the heavenly bodies."

"Well, as far as the cold and sunburn are concerned, we will use a concoction of herbs growing especially on the Palani hills. You can check out the details of the creams too." Thalaivar took a screenshot and Whatsapped the image.

"And you want to hire two astronaut trainers right away?"

"Yes, for the six months that our last circumambulation should take."

"We can manage that," Bezo replied, tapping on his iPad. "Now, let's come to the discount part — "

Thalaivar interrupted before Bezo could complete. "We do not want to reduce the ticket price by half. A 10% discount should suffice. Please let me have your SpaceZ bank details," he said, his finger pointing at the 'Submit' button of the funds' transfer form on his iPad.

"Well, thank you. A 75% advance is good enough," Bezo said with a wide smile.

"Would you like to see the ISRO agreement?"

"Not necessary; I trust you," Bezo said, the smile still lingering on his face. "There is just one other thing: food. I know Indians love their food. So, what would you like on the menu?"

"Vegetarian. Anything without eggs, fish, or meat."

"Well, of course," Bezo said. "I should have known."

**

Being stuck in a crowd, even if colorful, and in hot weather can be quite distasteful and disorienting; nobody can adapt to it at any point in time. After six months on the high seas, Rodolfo Hernandez was not excited at seeing the meandering groups of tonsured heads swarming the Palani temple, the vibrant noises at the colorful stalls, or tasting the sweet offering of mashed banana mixed with honey, dried fruits, and jaggery—the *Panchamritham*. He hopped onto the rough, rocky parapet and sat gazing gloomily at the misty green canopy downhill, not caring to discover how low down the forest was.

The task of the mission, thought Rodolfo, the very idea of it was insane. "Mission One-Way," it seemed some nut job back at the space center had named it. For months now, they had been sailing across oceans in the nauseating, old submarine, stopping at temples in Singapore, East Asia, the UK, and the US. At every stop, the Kavadis had been smearing sandalwood paste on their chests, lifting semicircular wooden structures, piercing cheeks and tongue, yelling chants, and dancing their way into the temples. As they had sailed, however, the team trained underwater for practicing movements in weightless conditions, worked in spacesuits, getting into and out of the outfit, using the launchpad, and learning the engineering mechanics.

This evening, if all went well, they would have completed the last of it. Just what sanctity did the Kavadis see in the number 108 and not the rounding off to 100 as in the decimal system, Rodolfo didn't know. Although not particularly fond of seas, he loved the adventure. But the mere thought of Thalaivar prolonging the rituals or increasing the circumambulations on a sudden spiritual vision sent an involuntary shudder down his spine. His mandate was to guide them back smoothly to the space station after the last circling and accost them to space until the drop. The upcoming special space launch was well organized and advertised widely. If they delay now, they would lose potential international customers.

A warm hand touched his arm and he turned to see Greg standing next to him. There was a dab of holy ash on his forehead. He was wearing a yellow *Veshti*—a sarong-like unstitched cloth—the Kavadis had gifted him, and licking the remnants of the *Panchamritham* off his palm. He, it seemed, was quite willing to adapt to their ways. In turn, he shared his evening drinks with them – a pleasure they did not abstain from. Once, the Kavadis got him piss-drunk with a local toddy and he couldn't recover for almost two days. One thing was sure: they might be tough and all with their spartan life, but they were not far from temptations.

"There are certain things happening here that I hope do not put us in trouble," whispered Greg excitedly.

"Are they canceling the trip? Did their supplies not arrive?" Rodolfo's words tumbled out before he could help it, while all the while he wished it were not true.

"Not like that," Greg said urgently, hopping onto the parapet. "I've just found out from the Kavadis what all this is about." He sat with a thud.

"Yeah," said Rudolfo with a sigh of relief. "We knew it all along: a human continuation of a local folklore."

"No, the reason for the one-way ticket," he asked.

"Suicidal mission—but a pretty expensive one at that, I must say." Rodolfo chuckled.

"Not like that," said Greg.

" —but, what else can you expect of these people following primitive ways; no one to call the emperor naked," growled Rodolfo.

"Thalaivar, you know the way he fell at the feet of the high Thalaivar in a trance. Then, he mumbled something about going out of air. The team is now sitting around a rectangular structure building the sacred fire. Chants are on in the choultry. The high Thalaivar is worshipping the fire with chants and clarified butter—and then, Thalaivar told me."

"Go on, I'm all ears."

"They are going to live in space after the launch."

"Are they extending their stay?"

"Not mere extension. It is forever."

"What? Are there no limits for this foolishness?" Rudolfo yelled. Belligerence tore into his face.

"Relax. Listen to this: they believe that when they have completed the 108 circumambulations – and they've just completed them today – they'll join the league of gods. The lower realms—the earth—will be destroyed soon. The Kavadis will evolve into breathless beings, so they can live outside the earth, in space."

"What breathless beings? You mean they'll die?" Rudolfo's bellicose voice boomed.

"No, he said they will be humans, flesh, blood and all, but without breathing air."

"How's that possible? You need oxygen to circulate the blood."

"There are beings which don't need to breathe. Like Loricifera, the microscopic animals living in the Mediterranean."

"And then, what are we, mere mortals, to do?" Rudolfo asked, helplessness seeping into his tone..

"Nothing. It'll be painless destruction, they said."

"So, after the fire ritual, living beings will begin falling down one by one?"

Greg tittered. "Not exactly. They said, after some time. And, we don't know when."

"Don't you see? It's a joke, that is all it is."

Rodolfo's flushed face eased out. After a pause, he said, "But these tribes are crazy, and we knew about that. There is nothing to do."

"Yes — but look at it like this: if they are as crazy as we think they are, and they do not end up being gods, how do we know they will not perish in space?"

Rudolfo looked upwards with his thumb and index finger resting on his chin. "Look, an apocalypse was predicted in 2012; the year came and went and nothing happened. They just thought it was a mistake. This ritual may also turn out to be one. However, ancient Celtic tribes in Britain had esoteric knowledge restricted to the Celtic priests who performed rituals to a pantheon of gods. They gave powerful blessings. Your grandparents were British. Surely, you'd know something about that."

"This mistake could cost them their lives. It could cost us our credibility. The company could shut down. I wish we had never taken up this mission."

"I was tired of it myself, right from the start. But, they did say they had adequate supplies and the emergency Indian spaceship. So, nothing to be done there."

Rudolfo, now thoughtful, resumed. "Or we could hang around near them until the ISRO spaceship arrived."

"Well, well, err —" Greg dragged on.

"What is it?"

"Hmm, now that's another thing I discovered. You know that toothless Kavadi, the one we nicknamed Huck? He told me there never was any agreement with ISRO or the supplies," Greg said with a nervous laugh.

Rudolfo's eyebrows furrowed. "But they were eager to show the agreement to Bezo; he swore by it. Then, why the lie?"

"It was a white lie. They had an agreement document alright, but it was about food supply."

"Well, then let us inform Bezo. And, why did you not tell me earlier?"

"Let us analyze the solution options and inform Bezo of the current scenario and the solutions. He can decide on the options that maximize our end of the deal.."

"Ok, the solution would be to tether them as in spacewalks, wait for their prayers, and drag them back in," said Rudolfo.

"Or we could drop them and let ISRO do the rest."

"We cannot collaborate with ISRO. If they ever knew about this, they might cancel the whole venture, which would turn out to be a real setback for us."

"In which case, depending on our supplies, we could shorten their prayer time. But, let me tell you one thing: I don't like where this is going."

"Yes, I don't like it a wee bit," said Rudolfo. "It'll be the first time a mission is getting so complicated and unpredictable with time. Let's call up Bezo."

After a few minutes, old Huck came out through the entrance smiling his toothless smile and waving. He looked at Rudolfo and Greg and said, "Thalaivar has requested your presence at the choultry. You are eligible for the blessings from the high Thalaivar as you joined them in the last circumambulation."

"Ah, I don't know," Rodolfo hesitated..

"What have we got to lose, anyway?" said Greg with a shrug.

"Well, in that case, could the high Thalaivar also bless our families through a video call?"

"No problem, anything you wish." Huck turned to go. Rudolfo and Greg followed.

**

"Lock it tight," said Rudolfo into his helmet boom mic four days later, as the last of the Kavadis walked out through the airlock. Collecting themselves between the airlock and the second door, the Kavadis checked their tethers before opening the second door to get out. He heard the hatch open.

"And behind all that nonchalant face, they hide foolish secrets as if we didn't know. Where are the blessed breathless beings? For all their conviction, I'm surprised they meticulously wore those special spacewalk spacesuits. How we had to hurry with those two extra spacewalk suits at the last minute. As if getting their suits ready were not impossible enough." Rudolfo tapped his forehead in disgust.

"I don't know why they can't come out clean," replied Greg. "Maybe they realized we would wait to take them back. Perhaps they didn't bother; maybe they are loaded with money." As the systems increased pressure, Greg felt the thumping of the valves' opening and closing.

Rudolfo looked at the extra layer of the life support system he had removed after seeing the Kavadis off; he didn't need them—at least not for a few hours now—inside the spaceship. From the window, he saw the Kavadis floating, hands folded in prayer. He heaved a sigh. This was the place chosen by the Kavadis for prayer. The spaceship was right on top of the Palani temple and moving at the earth's rotational speed so as to keep its position there. The position was equidistant from the two DSN antennas and had a declination value of near zero, that is, near the equator.

Rudolfo jumped to the pilot's seat in slow leaps. The expansive, dark space lay stretched in front: specks of light glittered, here and there, like fireflies in a forest. Thalaivar chose the 'holy' time to move out of the spaceship for the prayers—one o'clock in the afternoon. Rudolfo could not hide his frustration. He was resolving in his mind to never again travel with devout strangers.

He knew exactly what hymns they were muttering in their prayers. The Kavadis floated in a circle, and Thalaivar was standing in their midst. Had he not seen the rituals day in and day out in the submarine for all those six months? But, it was good they chose to circumambulate in a submarine. The training that would otherwise have been at the large Neutral Buoyancy Lab pool at NASA's space center in Texas was rendered at the natural sea, not to speak of the low expenses incurred as a result. The first thing he would do going home was to go to Florida on a long family holiday.

"Look!" cried Greg, pointing at the window. "They are removing the helmets."

Rudolfo involuntarily gritted his teeth. They were certainly capable of it. He knew he would not have a moment's peace with their antics. As he tried making giant leaps towards the airlock, he remembered that he had to put on the life support. Why did he remove it? Why was he so sure they would not do anything weird? Oh, how he could never forgive himself now.

"It'll take them four hours to remove it all," said Greg.

"That'll give me four hours to wear. If I wear it faster, I can catch them before they run away." Rudolfo moved his legs fast. "Alert the ground station right away," he commanded Greg.

"If they are unshackling the tether the last, that's good," commented Greg after radioing the emergency alert.

It was now almost three in the afternoon. They'd been praying right on top of their holy temple for the last two hours. Perhaps their plan was to perish right on top of it to transform into gods—only time could tell. Unfortunately for them, Rudolfo would not allow it. He would step out as would Greg and drag them back into the safe oxygen of the spaceship. He had had enough. What he had feared the most had finally happened. Now, there was no more fear. If not all, they would save at least two fellow humans.

He began to talk constantly into the helmet mic, which he had put on first. The voice messages that he was getting from the ground station were swift and brief: object velocity and location. But, Rudolfo knew that when spaceships were themselves a 'pale blue dot' on the station's screens, humans would be next to invisible.

The atomic clock struck six. "Ready?" asked Rudolfo.

"The Kavadis have disappeared. They were real fast," screamed Greg.

Rudolfo immediately instructed the pilot to stay on course. He clicked the airlock hatch open. Greg followed. They spent about a minute before the second door praying for luck.

"Hope they've not finished removing," said Rudolfo, looking back over his shoulders. "Wonder if they had gone breathless by now," he added, managing a nervous laugh.

Greg didn't reply. Rudolfo gripped the hatch of the second door. He turned around to see Greg's eyes closed in prayer.

"Oh, come on now!" He roared. "I'm going to open the door."

Greg opened his eyes slowly. "Look," he whispered, removing his gloves. Rudolfo saw him lifting his helmet and moving his index finger near his nose. Greg rubbed his hands with glee.

Opening the second door, Rudolfo suddenly looked up. A sparkling meteor shower caught his eyes. It was radiating farther in the heavens. In the next instant, his breath stopped.

Arms outstretched, the Kavadis, without much ado, greeted him with a happy, warm smile.

***

II

Breaking Point

Meenakshi heard the raspy heaving in her son's chest while the nasal prongs were tubed to a brand new oxygen cylinder. Ram's breathing may get steadier soon. She held the wi-fi thermometer to his forehead until Alexa's synthetic voice enunciated his temperature. The vibration frequencies had been precisely set. Her sonification research was the only hope left for her to revive him.

At first, he gasped desperately, hands holding hers tightly and crouching with bent shoulders. As desperate as her first son Venkat had been after a stuffy nose turned into an incessant cough and an unbearable wheeze. She had braced herself up to get him tested for the Covid-19 infection. The results being a dreadful positive, the screening center had checked him for severity of symptoms when the doctors finalized on a hospitalized treatment. It wasn't until a few days later that Venkat's condition worsened, and he was shifted to the ICU.

Touching the table by his bedside, Meenakshi set the ultrasonic vibration exciter on top. It could become worse before it becomes better. She recalled. After a moment, the creaking sounds of Ram's recliner bed alerted her, and she smiled. Reclined like Venkat when he was moved back to the regular Covid-19 ward. Meenakshi spoke to her friend, a nurse at the Covid-19 center, and she assured Venkat would recover soon. He was a healthy, strong lad of seventeen who had grown out of childhood asthma long back. Once, she had sneaked into the ward, all dressed in a PPE, holding the nurse's hand, and caressed Venkat's forehead while he was asleep, hoping he would be back home that week.

Squeaking sounds emanated from the bed followed by the swooshing of garments. Ram got up and wriggled out of the prongs. His breathing was normal, but there was strange silence.

"Where am I?" He asked.

He sounded confused. Meenakshi was left confused when Venkat was moved again into the ICU the day she was assured he would be discharged from the ward. Even when the nurse tried to convince her that Venkat's lungs were perforated by the virus, she asked how then had he gotten better. The doctor had her sign Venkat on for experimental drugs, promising he would do his best. She didn't know the doctors and nurses were exhausted, and the health workers fell short of the necessary training required to handle infectious patients.

Now Ram was coughing continuously in an effort to bring out a particularly hard mucus. The way Venkat did, long and hard coughing and eventually bringing up something black, the nurse said was black fungus. That was during his last day at the regular ward. Until then he was laughing and talking with gay abandon. Meenakshi had greeted him that day but received only coughs in reply. Standing in the direction of the cough sound, her throat had choked, and tears welled up in her eyes. She tried to dissuade the ICU shifting, and the nurse supported her too. Meenakshi wondered if the oxygen cylinder containers at the hospital were rusted and humid.

Ram brought it out finally. His footsteps sounded past her, pausing to the sounds of water gushing and a stiff spit, and starting again to stop with a body thud on the bed. When the nurse called her to inform her of Venkat's death, she had fallen on her bed with a thud. How could he recover from Covid-19 but succumb to black fungus? Outside the quarantine ward, Meenakshi tried to talk to the doctors—they maintained that the perforation was due to the virus and not the fungus.

Ram coughed again, then took a deep breath and a few sharp breaths, contracting his chest. He stretched his palm, placing it flat onto his chest. He exhaled in quick successions. Meenakshi turned in the direction of the breath sounds and approached him, exciter in hand. While he slept, she had adjusted the frequencies again to 360° sweep and a frequency range set as the first-order bending frequencies at ultrasonic levels. These frequencies were proved to break the virus that has a protein cell layer by vibrating it long enough to shatter its chemical bond. A direct contact of the exciter to the chest would inactivate the virus. All that was left was to embed the right combination of frequencies resonant enough to combat the ever-changing and mutating virus inside the body.

Ram lay flat on the bed, his mother tying up concave audio speakers on the railings of the recliner. She picked up the exciter and positioned it a little above his lung area. Ram moved his torso unevenly but assured his mother he didn't feel any pain. He was merely scared of the new form of cure. Just like how Meenakshi was scared of the new turmoil the world was going through, which brought death in an abnormal way and clearly unpredictable. Unprepared to face the sudden death in her family, and that too of her child, she felt extremely painful at the thought of outliving her own child. Where was the question of holding any medical personnel accountable in those turbulent times in May 2021 when the delta variant was killing loads of Indians? She was not allowed to touch him; not allowed anywhere near his body; not allowed into the hospital, and definitely not allowed at the special cremation grounds. The worst, she couldn't even see the ambulance that drove him away.

So, she put her astrophysics background to good use. Having had to switch from astronomer to the sonification field owing to diminishing eyesight, Meenakshi began a sonic experiment to treat Covid-19 when Venkat caught the seemingly mild flu.

The nurse had forged an ID badge and dressed her up in the PPEs. Amidst the panic-stricken crowd around the government hospital, the only Covid-19 care center in Chennai city, and overworked police and medical personnel, security wouldn't notice her any more than the patient on the next bed to Ram's. Then Ram was escorted out in a PPE by the nurse holding Meenakshi's hand on the other side. Most importantly, they went to Meenakshi's workshop space in the suburbs of Chennai, a fairly desolated area. It was the same unpleasant decision of the doctors to shift Venkat back to the ICU, now for Ram, that propelled Meenakshi to kidnap her own son.

Ram had a chance at revival. In fact, he was only getting better when there was a sudden dip. The nurse had ruled out the black fungus. But Meenakshi did not trust the hospital. She was frantically working away at the software that fed the frequencies into the exciter. The agony of not having been able to save her child left her miserable. As the bending strength of the spike protein of the virus was not known, she assumed that of common steel—300 MPa—the maximum megapascal beyond which the virus would lose its ability to hold on to human cells. Tapping away furiously to insert the length of the RNA of the virus, she modeled the virus for testing her software. The day she brought back Ram, she hit upon the right resonant frequency range: 9 – 16 Hz, at least in theory and testing.

Corporation health workers who were paid to catch hiding Covid-19 cases were furiously tracking every house of their designated areas. It was easier to bribe them earlier, but now with stringent rules, the option was totally gone. The nurse, however, drawn to Meenakshi's plight and justified action, did her best. A patient resembling Ram was replaced by the deft nurse on the bed, medical notes at the foot of the bed switched.

While a research assistant for the Astrophysics department at the Madras University, Meenakshi had taken up turning astrophysical data into sound. When stars produce burning gases, the heat changes push the gases as sounds push the air on earth. Sound waves were thus produced by these explosive events. The pitch of the sound waves translated to recognizable notes. Meenakshi was collaborating with a music composer to convert imagery to music. But the soothing stellar music memory was now torture for her when she felt a certain deep anxiety about her helplessness in curing her son.

After what seemed like ages, Ram finally took a deep breath. His chest mucus was clearing, but he had to alternate between sitting up and lying flat. The fight between the virus and the vibration was on. Sometimes he took short breaths and had to sit up, sometimes he sobbed, sometimes he lay with relief after the cough sessions, and other times he sighed with heaviness. Meenakshi had cried many times in the last few months. After what seemed a long struggle, his tone finally sounded bright. Now she smiled.

The nurse checked Ram's vitals and patted Meenakshi after giving her a relieved hug. A week's mess was waiting for her to clean up around the workshop: half-eaten pizzas, opened canned food, stray clothes, and wires running around the equipment.

"Amma!" He said. Meenakshi noticed how strong her son's voice was. Maskless and shieldless, she hugged him tight and kissed him all over the face. And here he would make a sound recovery, inaudible winning over invisible.

***

III

The Power of Zero

Any object is either present or absent. Duality is prevalent in everything as opposites: air and space; sound and silence; and everything and nothing, or so it seems. However, in reality, the earth so full of objects and surrounded by air hangs in invisible space; sounds discernible to the human ear are part of a spectrum of inaudible frequencies otherwise known as silence. The all-inclusive nothingness reigns supreme, and the key to which lies in the human heart; therefore, unlocking it evolves the mind.

In 1993, on a new moon day in August, a Chinese family had prostrated in front of a levitating Tibetan monk surrounded by burning candles to the guttural, low-pitched, and unvarying drone-like chants in the Drepung monastery—the day that defined the destiny of their three-year-old grandson, Wang Yi. With great reverence for the spiritual Himalayan kingdom, the old Chinese Kung-fu fighter had strongly nudged his son's family to come along to seek the monk's holy blessings.

When Wang Yi stood awestruck, breathless but scared stiff, the monk had opened his eyes and motioned him to come close. He strode like a pro, lifted his face as told, and received writing on his forehead with an inkless nib of a peacock feather. Outside, the yellow sun shone bright, rays parting through thick cumulus clouds on the majestic Himalayan kingdom. Eyes lit with wonder and lips beaming a proud smile, the fighter had gone on to say," See, how calm my grandson is—the first step to courage; he will be a great warrior-seer one day."

Not a day passed without Wang recollecting about the levitating monk. Now 32, he could still remember every detail of the experience: monastery nestled at the foot of snow-capped mountains surrounded by the clear and turquoise Namtso lake, rich, deep tones produced by the singing bowls, the bang of large meditation gongs, the low, respectful talk of the tourists, the fading of the sounds, the appearance of the monk counting the prayer beads, the slow rising of the meditative mendicant who sat still at two feet above the ground. But, no one dared guess what the monk had written on his forehead, not even Wang.

The twilight sky shimmered with the crimson sun in the far west, and colorful Virginia's autumnal tree tops looking like mushrooms covered the land all the way to the horizon. When the long holographic video call to his wife ended, Wang cautioned her not to rush with enthusiasm and cover bomb-raided areas and prodded her to return soon. Blowing her a loving goodbye kiss, he removed the periscope mounted on his smartphone. From the Stone Mountain's Observation tower, staring at the expanse, Wang sulked when nagging thoughts about his destiny returned—for the nth time. He was in the US working with NASA, was that what was written—was that it? An everyday life of coding, fixing bugs and errors, and finding solutions to recurring issues—all that only to run machines built for projects and missions. Maybe he could have been an astronaut or a scientist in the space and meteorology department at the organization—but as a child in Beijing, he had enrolled in computer classes like everyone else and excelled in it nonetheless. Later, bored of computers, he ran away to join the Shaolin monastery. He excelled there too. But then again, contrary to the monastery rules, he fell in love. His American wife lived in Washington. There, he sat at her home for a few months training himself on the latest coding languages, procured a Google certificate, and joined NASA. Absorbed in his thoughts, he did not notice crimson turning to maroon; maroon to deep red. Only a thin piece of the sphere was seen above the horizon. Coming to the US could not be a destiny, could it? Lots of people migrated. Wang could not stop feeling a tinge of disappointment. Maybe he took the prophecy too seriously. Maybe he should not have left the Shaolin monastery. Or maybe the monk was teaching him humility. Maybe he had to just be a non-entity and learn to contend with being an ordinary person. A deep thirst for something substantial had set in. His life till now was fragmented although the parts were a whole in themselves: the part of being a Shaolin monk could have extended to his whole life had he continued, and the part of being a coder now might be life in itself. Wang missed the connecting thread. The ex-Shaolin monk focussed on the falling sun. Could his destiny be greater than the sum of its parts?

A thinking mind is a weak mind, they taught him that, the monks. But here he was slicing and dicing his past and not able to reconcile with his fate. Wang sighed. Taking a deep breath, he visualised wiping his mind clean and focussed again on the horizon. The mind quietened, he looked up at the greying sky. The colorful canopy below was looking dim. Dusk was slowly enveloping the expanse all around him. Wang's eyelids dropped for a split second and would have stayed closed if not for a speck of light shining above the canopy. His senses getting into a hyper-alert mode, Wang opened his eyes fully. Another speck of light glowed on his right. Before he could turn his head, another one followed. Here one, there one; all in split seconds.

At first, Wang dismissed it as fireflies or blinking lights of an aircraft. His mind processed fast. The color was not yellow nor was there a buzzing sound of an aircraft accompanying it, even if from afar.

The specks played hide and seek, and too fast at that. Were there many such specks? Or only one moving real fast? To an ordinary mind, it looked dazzling and one too many. But the Shaolin-trained still, focussed and quick mind sensed the nanosecond gap between the specks. Yes, it was only one but it looked like many. Descending into the forest below, ripping off the top of trees, it burrowed into a large crate. Despite the sky glowing dark in the dusk, Wang scanned the speck of light that turned out to be a headlight, below which the silhouette of a pitch-black, large hemispherical spacecraft appeared floating above the canopy.

**

Weren't aliens a myth, perpetrated by the Americans—as if there weren't enough problems already? Wang couldn't believe his eyes. It was dark, but Wang took a quick snap from his smartphone with the night vision camera on. There is no harm in exploring a little, is there? From 4000 feet above, it would take at least 10 minutes to drive down; another 15 minutes, maybe, to reach the spot; and then God knows how long to enter the spacecraft. He called his boss. It was Sunday evening, the ring went on until it rang no more; he must be drunk or lying somewhere half-naked.

In a now-or-never manner, he called up JPL, the R&D lab at Caltech. Anne, a dedicated researcher, picked up the call. Wang sent her images of the spacecraft. The military and scientist teams were called in. The images made their way to the director of the lab, then to the US Military, and finally to the Defence Minister.

"Every day, some tramp or the other spots a UFO and tries to create panic. Let's first find out the authenticity and then inform the President," so saying the minister dismissed his secretary.

The speck served as his guiding light. Expecting to bump on a metal surface anytime, Wang drove carefully near the light. Slipping the smartphone and periscope into his pant pockets, he left the car and trod on the soft forest grounds. The phone's torch light shone on a dark metallic surface about 50 meters away. He took snaps. But to his surprise, the surface ended halfway hanging in the air. When he moved the light up and down, he could not see the bottom half of the spacecraft. It was probably floating or not landed yet, he thought. He took more snaps. Now, he could walk directly below it and take more snaps, he thought. But, when he strode right in the middle, he hit himself hard on the metallic surface. Rubbing his head, he let out a scowl. What was that? A spy app with infrared rays detected the lower half of the spacecraft. Wow, one half was visible and another, invisible. He ran to a nearby tree, hid behind the trunk, and called up the lab to report and send fresh snaps.

Were the spacecraft to stand instead of lie across the land, it would stand taller than the pyramids, thought Wang, recording through his phone camera—now, on video mode—across its length. Dwarf-sized beings floated out of it carrying large metal crates like shipping containers. They looked human: a face, two eyes, two ears, one nose, two hands, chest, and hip. He saw no legs. He sensed their hips move as if they walked but couldn't see them walk. It took only two dwarf-aliens to lift and move a one-tonne container. Wang was stunned and scared for the second time in his life. They opened the crates and closed them after a few minutes. He pressed the audio record button. One by one, they returned to their spacecraft. The NASA or military teams should be here in the next hour or so.

Wang sneaked into one of the containers. Upon inspection, there was nothing in it, nothing. He managed to slip out just in time before it got closed. The dwarf-aliens moved their mouths, but no sounds came out. They seemed to understand each other. Baffled on what the stealth spacecraft full of dwarf-aliens without legs was stealing, Wang continued taking snaps as that's all he could do then.

An hour passed by, and still no sign of the teams. The dwarf-aliens loaded the spacecraft to their satisfaction in less than an hour, contrary to Wang's estimate that it would take all night, closed the door, and left as surreptitiously as they had arrived. Wang stood bewildered, right under the spacecraft as it rose. How come nobody saw it? Of the 7.9 billion people in the world, not one except me noticed it? What of the astronomers?—the satellites, the defense radars, the air traffic controllers, or even the amateurs—where were they all? Now, how would anyone believe me?

Exactly like the police car sirens that would arrive after the climax in Hollywood movies, the teams' cars raced to a roaring halt. The US Army Captain Osborne hopped out, tripped, stood chin up first, and then looked sideways to ensure nobody noticed his misstep. Even the President had stumbled up the stairs to the aircraft, thinking he chuckled. Changing into a rigid posture and sharp eyes, he screamed orders to secure the perimeter. Wang expected to see a pair of F-22 fighters slice across the sky, at least. All that was left now was the emptied-out elliptical shape on crushed trees and his multitude of snaps. The experts set out collecting any alien remains that they might have inadvertently left behind.

**

Uploading the images on a SoC (all types of computers: CPUs, GPUs, and DSPs on a chip) platform at JPL, Anne ran an object detection program. The tags on the results: 200-meter long spacecraft, 40-ft long containers, trees, leaves, clothes, and 2-ft dwarf-aliens standing on unidentifiable lines. She scratched her head.

The video recording was played on a large monitor in the conference room where other JPL and defense researchers sat observing every tiny frame. There was no movement in the sound spectrograph. The lack of audio was perplexing, as were the floating dwarves. They wore yellow robes across their chests covering one side of it. The robe seemed bunched and secured around their hips making the viewers suspect the possibility of legs. None of them wore glasses but had long hair tied in tufts with some down to their hips. Their lips moved in the manner of speaking, but nothing could be heard, and they never spoke much. While working, they exuded a certain calmness that stretched till the end of the tasks—no hurry and certainly no excitement—as if all of them were in control of the situation all the time. The clock struck twelve. Amazed and puzzled, the tired teams decided to sleep on it.

At dawn, coffee in hand, Wang set up an ultrasonic detector to take in the feed from the video recording. To his pleasant surprise, the monitor showed wave movements. In another breakthrough, he ran a combination of neural nets in the ultrasonic domain and detected the legs of the dwarf-aliens. A combination with infrared did not work. He found it strange and concluded that there was perhaps no heat generated in their bodies.

They wore black pants. So, the dwarf-aliens were 4 ft tall – two ft upper body and 2 ft lower body, only one half of the body was visible. That was like their spacecraft, which was half-visible. Wang took a few minutes to take it all in. He did not update his journalist wife, who was halfway around the globe covering the war-laden Afghanistan. No one in the teams was supposed to update their spouses, no leak to the media too. It was a secret mission, that is at least until they figured out the threats and solutions.

The teams went debating on what the dwarf-aliens would have stolen. Wang swore he went in and out and found nothing. But, as the pattern of nothing seemed to be filled with something only discovered through ultrasonics and infrared, the experts wanted to run the images through every detector device the lab had. Still, they ended up with nothing.

The sonic weapons military team converted the ultrasonic frequencies to audible levels. In the 45-minute recording, hardly a few words were spoken. But they were clear words with pauses in between resembling a sentence or two. Their expressions were similar to humans—just more subdued. The experts finally zeroed in on two sentences: one, Nangal ela deinde amavasya; and second, abeamus pros to saubha.

Linguistic experts opined that the words came from four ancient languages: Latin, Greek, Tamil, and Sanskrit.

Nangal (Tamil) - We will

Ela(Greek) - return

Diende(Latin) - next

Amavasya(Sanskrit) - New Moon day

Abeamus(Latin) - Let's go

Piso(Greek) - back

Saubha(Sanskrit) - Spaceship

So, their sentences were a mixed bag of the four old-world languages. It was possible, they said that Saubha may not translate to a spaceship but the name of the spaceship. The captain named the operation: Mission Saubha.

**

"So much for our hi-tech intelligence!" The defense minister slammed the report the teams had painstakingly made. "Why could you not figure out the location where the dwarf-aliens would attack next?"

With his calloused hands, Captain Osborne saluted. "The dwarf-aliens did not speak much. Spotting a communication and retrieving the two sentences was in itself a miracle," he said.

"Now, I've to alert Russia, China, UK, France, Germany, Japan, and a whole horde of other nations. Maybe India too," the minister barked. "And, God alone knows how messy it'll be," he added.

"I'm sorry, sir, but the only way to detect Saubha would be to activate the ultrasonic sensors in all the satellites surrounding the earth. That way, we would be able to see the exact location it will land on," he said.

The minister frowned. "What weapons have we ready that could be transported to the location in a few minutes' time?"

"We've NASA X-15 fighters that would at 4000 mph take hardly 6 minutes to reach the other end of the earth. The missiles can destroy a satellite. For the 200-meter-long Saubha, we could send 15 fighters which could deliver missiles simultaneously to explode it."

"Send them before Saubha enters our atmosphere. It should be destroyed before setting its foot on our planet. All the best." The boisterous minister dismissed the captain wondering why they, the Americans, were so fearful to panic at the drop of a pin. Too much prosperity for too long.

Beijing lined up its stealth drones and fighters, killer missiles, and electromagnetic railguns; Moscow assembled its unmanned vehicles and artillery; the UK put together its special air service weapons; Germany drew up its anti-aircraft weapons, and France prepared its Rafales. India waited and watched.

**

The new moon day arrived, finally. It was in the month of August 2022.

Captain Osborne set up a trailer where several offices were separated by thin layers of tented material. Through the bay of various monitor stations of NASA scientists, military researchers, communication experts, diplomats, and state department representatives, Wang was seen standing at one satellite feed flatscreen monitor, talking to a Chinese man from the Beijing military station. Elsewhere, a group of scientists watched British teams explain the signals from their satellites. Three bunks over, on a screen, the Russian site was displaying the evening sky over Kamchatka.

A blip on Wang's station sent a tense hush throughout the trailer. Latitude: 11.63S; Longitude: 169.83E; Location: Anuta near the Solomon Islands, South Pacific. So, it was true; what Wang had said was true; the images were real—everyone let out a gasp. The captain slapped his forehead: of all the places on earth, they had to choose this one. Wang's sharp mind made a quick calculation: they chose an island this time, the reason being isolation and plenty of pure air. The dwarf-aliens seemed to know what they were doing, he said. Very smart and tricky too.

An eruption of chaos with several diplomats talking at once to their monitors and a flurry of activities went on. Over the commotion when everyone ran around frantically, and nobody listened, came the captain's booming voice, "Alert the naval chief and send the submarines."

"Nobody should share this information with our enemies." A CIA agent added.

A lieutenant entered, "The Secretary of Defense is on the line," he saluted the captain. A moment later, he yelled, "The Chinese have reached the spot."

"Shall I suggest sending our fighter aircraft?" Wang asked. Captain Osborne nodded and gave commands. Interrupting him, Wang urged the captain to let him participate too. With a call to the Defense Secretary, the captain recommended Wang's presence in the fighter plane—the Air Force Chief could not refuse. Keeping down the receiver, he said, "We'll try to squeeze you in, but it is unofficial. We are not responsible for your safety.".At the same time, the special forces dashed off into the line of fighter aircraft parked at The Boneyard.

Leaving behind the frenzied trailer, Wang, armed with noise-canceling headphones, night vision goggles, and ultrasonic sensors in his mobile, flew to the Anuta island seated next to the pilot as an observer, An explosion near the island lit up the shores like the plume of a fire cloud. Wang noticed a Chinese ship bombing. On the island at the far end, he caught sight of Saubha through the goggles. Unmindful of the blasts, the dwarf-aliens seemed to do the job as they did the last time. His pilot launched a missile. The dwarf-aliens still went about their work as if nothing had happened.

Wang's feed showed armed Chinese soldiers landing on the shores to a background of the noise of incessant gunfire. Their ships surrounded the island behind which were the submarines. The American and Russian fighter aircrafts edged into view. Navigation panels showed wilderness where a large, hemispherical object hovered over a tree line. They launched missiles. Wang compelled the pilot to let him land. Nimbly navigating the island, he reached the spot where Saubha stood. To the radius of 100 meters, there were no shots heard, no explosions, and certainly no bomb blasts. The place was as quiet as dead; the dwarf-aliens went about opening and closing the metal containers. *How could it be? The whole island was burning, but Saubha and an area of 100 meters around was so immune?* The bullets, missiles, and bombs simply bounced off the area. Bewilderment seized him. Wang observed a group of Russian, American, and Chinese forces moping into the area. At first glance, Wang figured out that they held the latest Chinese sonic guns. That was really clever of them—the Chinese—he thought. Non-lethal though, the shots delivered infrasounds (inaudible – lower than 20 hertz) that could affect the mental balance of the dwarf-aliens. But, those too failed miserably. At that moment, he knew that no amount of artillery or creative weapons could hurt them.

Back on his feet within moments, he realised that if nothing happened in the next hour or so, they would lose the dwarf-aliens again. With a quick move, he swiftly ran towards one container where a dwarf alien was resting, pressed his hand against its mouth, tied the hands, and carried him to the fighter plane. He heard the violent shots fade as the aircraft flew back. From the plane's rearview mirror, he sensed the possibility of Saubha rising up amidst large flames with thick, choking fumes. His goggles confirmed it.

**

From their spy satellite feed, the Indians watched the once peaceful and pristine island ablaze and burn with sky-high flames. Why couldn't the Chinese do their homework and then confront, the Indian Defense Minister wondered? Rash and reckless; never growing up. For that matter, all the superpowers believed in aggression as their only weapon to stay safe. If you want peace, go to war—the Western principle based on a Latin adage that shaped their approach to living or rather conquering. For all the Chinese tall talk of not being influenced by the western civilization, they are the first ones to adopt everything, including opera, the minister sighed. Updating the Prime Minister, he said, "Sir, our man on the ground will do it all. I've complete faith." The PM smiled. He remembered how the Pandavas only requested the presence of Lord Krishna—that too, unarmed—and the Kauravas demanded the lord's army in the eternal Mahabharata epic's great war; the rest was history.

The minister grabbed the remote and turned the set to CNN, revealing live aerial footage of the island from a helicopter as a reporter narrated in near panic: forest fires consumed the island and its primitive inhabitants.

On his way back to the trailer, Wang had to hug the dwarf alien tight for lack of space. It kicked him all the way with its invisible legs. Underneath his arms, it felt cold. It wasn't breathing when Wang shut its mouth on the island. It wasn't breathing still, yet it winked, its body moved, and it kicked. Wang had recently read about the only creature on earth that did not breathe, possibly the only one—Loricifera. Found at the bottom of the Mediterranean, the microscopic animals did not have a circulatory system but reproduced. But it lived in the water, not on land. Maybe the alien was its land counterpart, thought Wang.

To thunderous claps from the teams, Wang escorted the dwarf-alien into a rectangular chamber with semi-transparent walls. Wang quickly set up an arsenal of audio, video, and other ultrasonic-enabled recording devices including UV and IR cameras and an old-tech sound spectrograph in his office. He caught a few winks of sleep afterwards. It was best to sleep when the dwarf-alien slept.

At eight in the morning, the trailer was abuzz with silent awe. Leading the dwarf-alien escorted by the lieutenants and the captain, Wang winded his way through a sea of monitors to his office. In a booth with an ultrasonic mic attached to a headset around it, for the first time, Wang beheld the dwarf-alien in sunlight. Sitting near Wang, the captain squinted his eyes and leaned in hoping to catch the sight of its legs. No luck there for both Wang and the captain.

Wang spoke into his mic: What is your name? 24 times. A permutation of the four words in the four languages. The sound waves were sent to the dwarf-alien headsets converted to ultrasonic frequencies.

No response.

It removed the headset and wore it again. For a moment, everything was quiet. Wang looked at the captain, the captain looked at him.

The sound spectrograph registered no frequencies. And then it moved his lips, the spectrograph spiked. The EMFISIS, an instrument suite translating electromagnetic waves called plasma waves into audible sound waves, recorded the response.

Vyushitaswa

The first exchange with an alien—a historic moment. Wang needed a pause. Flustered and with tearful eyes, Wang responded with gratitude, "I'm Wang. Let me call you Wu."

Wu nodded his head.

Straightening himself, Wang asked, "Why are you here?"

Get fresh air

The captain laughed; the smart alien needed more prodding.

"Elaborate," Wang said.

No air on our planet, so taking some air.

Wang could not believe his ears. Even the captain rolled his eyes. So, that was the mystery of the empty containers. The duo looked at each other.

"But you don't breathe," Wang said. Captain Osborne looked at him curiously.

A scientist had taken control of a video camera and held it at an angle that captured the lip movement of the alien.

Remember Loricifera? You thought about that organism on the aircraft.

Wang was taken aback. How did the alien know his thoughts? For a moment, stumped, Wang did not react. Gathering his senses, he said, "So, was that what you were filling in those containers?—Air?"

That is until you came along to foil our attempts.

"Still, that doesn't answer: why air when you are not breathing?"

Wu shifted uneasily in the chair. A lieutenant aimed his gun, but Wu gave a jerky laugh. Wang spoke into another ordinary mic to tell the lieutenant not to put a pistol to Wu's head—it was no use; holding him with his hands did the trick, he said. The bullets would simply bounce off Wu.

"Why?" Demanded Wang, yelling into the special mic.

Our planet is in the Andromeda galaxy. We lived well breathing fresh air on Gilese, our planet. We are what you'd call a transition to Super Humans; we were at least twelve feet tall; one-half of our bodies invisible—at will—to you Earthlings. We would have become fully invisible, but, around 108 years back, the air on Gilese started vanishing. To adapt, we resorted to the process of devolution, shrunk to a third of our size. with our powers. But, if we do not replenish Gilese soon, our living forms and race would be wiped out completely, nor would we be able to evolve back to our original height and powers.

"If we let you have our air, we will be wiped out soon enough," quipped Wang.

Wu turned its face in mock indignation.

"How did you discover the earth?"

We set out with the only spaceship we had, Saubha. It is a beauty we built to set sail in space. We have sailed for a year to reach the earth. The answer to how is: random discovery and luck.

"And a month to get back; in fact, 15 days each way?"

We upped the speed. The joy of laying our hands on air aided in speeding too.

"Really?"

Ok, celestial architect, Vishwakarma improved Saubha

"When do you attack next?" Wang asked.

And, why would I say that?

"Because you will not get your food."

I don't need your food or any food for that matter.

"By now, I can imagine that you eat gravitational waves for food, don't you? So, whenever hungry, you had hopped onto a planet and had your fill. Earth has it everywhere, so you don't need to. What if I put you on a spaceship and throw you out into space? You'll die hungry. I can do that," challenged Wang.

Next new moon day.

"We know that by now. Where?"

The Himalayas

**

The next few sessions consisted of the NASA scientists eliciting simple arithmetic concepts from Wu. Although their numerical system had numbers ranging from 1–9, there was no 10. Instead there was a zero. They said all the numbers were part of 0. Their computational systems were not based on the on-off theory of electricity, the 0, 1, but on nanosystem. What Earthlings perceived as opposites were not really their opposites, but parts of the whole—that whole symbolised as zero. At first, it seemed absurd, but if the dwarf-aliens had made trips to galaxies, the experts hoped to understand something out of it.

The teams huddled in the conference room discussing strategies to destroy Saubha and the dwarf-aliens. None of the current weapons however advanced, including sonic weapons, could vanquish them. There was no torture technique that would work on Wu. Plain questioning and answering, and that if and when Wu felt like it. The experts realised that Wu responded better to Wang. He seemed to like him. But, Wu was always one step ahead of Wang. He could read Wang's thoughts a few nanoseconds before Wang himself thought his thoughts. Wang was never sure if Wu planted his thoughts in Wang or simply read Wang's thoughts before they came to Wang.

The pressure on Wang to extract ways to destroy Wu and his group increased day by day. In a special session with Wang, once when Wang questioned him in Wu's booth, Wu was particularly silent. After a while, he struck Wang's heart with the tip of his index finger; an electric shock pierced him.

The next day, Wang cajoled him with questions about his family. When Wang asked about his sons and daughters. Wu fell from his chair. The lieutenants straightened him. Wang asked again. Wu fell to the side as if he had been slapped. Finally, Wang's face glowed as if he had learned the secret.

A long table adoring the Kennedy conference room in the White House headed by the secretary of defense seating Wang, Captain Osborne, NASA scientists, researchers, and military experts stood with a large monitor embedded on the wall behind the secretary.

"The dwarf-aliens have mastered the art of surrounding themselves with ultrasonic vibrations. Of course, they speak in them too. The ultrasonic aura levitates anything on its surface thus disorienting the object. That was the reason why no bullets or bombs could pierce, least of all blast or strike," Wang dived into the subject without any introduction.

"Have they built such a powerful aura that even missiles could not penetrate? What about nuclear missiles?" The secretary asked.

"Ultrasonics have become second nature to them. They are powerful in an internal way. That is, they do not hold external weapons, however mass-destructive. This is the ultimate way to weaponise oneself."

"What is the way out?"

"You could call it serendipity. In one of the questions, I mixed my voice with the ultrasonic—not my normal speaking voice but a touch of guttural, drone-like voice. It was accidental. But it served the purpose. No more fusion or fission causing fire for attacks. Only sonic attacks."

"So, what do you have in mind?"

"We need to find a large gathering of people who specialise in guttural speaking."

"Tuvan?" The captain suggested.

"That is more like whistling, it should be low tonal and drone-like. This kind of speaking sparks a mix of sonic and ultrasonic waves." Wang said.

"What is your proposal?" The secretary asked.

"Tibetan Buddhist monks chant in this way for hours together. We could round them up. It is also convenient that they live near the next attack location," Wang said.

"I'll have to speak with the Chinese Premier," the secretary said.

It took an hour-long phone call for the US President to convince the Chinese Premier to allow them to contact the Buddhist monks in Tibet. Wang spoke to the Drupang monastery head. The talks failed. The head was emphatic on the point that they would not chant without the Dalai Lama, and that the Chinese Premier had to respect and request him.

"Isn't it a matter of national, err.., international security? Please convince the Chinese Premier again," the secretary told the President.

"I don't believe Tibet is holy. Anyway, whatever holiness was left of it was wiped out when it became an armament base five or six decades ago," said the Chinese Premier.

"Our research with Wu clearly showed that the chants are our only chance of survival."

"This is yet another of your devious ways to curb my country's mightiness."

"Please understand. I am least bothered about Tibet. But, right now, we have no choice."

"Send me Wu. I need to test the theory myself," said the Chinese Premier.

**

Third attack: 25 September 2022

Around 400,000 Tibetan Buddhist monks gathered in Lhasa at the Potala Palace. An ensemble of the Dharma drums, cloud-shaped gongs, and large Brahma bells sat on the outer ring greeting the 86-year-old Dalai Lama's arrival. He was specially airlifted from India, personally greeted by the Chinese Premier on arrival, and seated on the Lion Throne at the center of the congregation. From the palace, Wang saw the last of the Chinese troops leaving the city.

Soldiers from all countries guarded Lhasa. Every country set up military camps complete with fighter aircraft in the mountains surrounding the city. Despite arguing about the futility, the defense heads of the countries said that they should be prepared in case the dwarf-aliens attacked the monks.

At 3:30 AM, the chanting began. Producing multiple distinct pitches, the throat-singing chants amplified the monks' voices. Repeated chants of Om Mani Padme hum were heard at regular intervals. The six syllables meant transforming from impurity to purity through wisdom. More than the meaning, the importance of mantras lay in the effect the micro frequencies emanating from the utterances of the syllables had on the listeners. The mixed sound waves penetrated every part of the earth's atmosphere to the magnetosphere layer.

In Beijing, Wu felt queasy. His aura began diminishing and his legs grew visible. With his vanishing powers went his memory and wisdom too. No use to the Chinese or anyone for that matter, the Chinese guards beamed at the prospect of torturing him to death. Fear hitherto unknown to Wu till then gripped him. A few weird guys tore at his body to eat it thinking they could get some powers too. Warding off the freaks, the Chinese Defense Minister gave Wu a decent cremation.

At dusk, Saubha descended. Opening the door, all the dwarf-aliens walked out with their containers. There was no iota of suspicion among them. Perhaps Wu did not transmit any thought waves, surmised Wang. The sonically charged atmosphere made a dent in Saubha—proof of Saubha's aura falling. Watching the feed, however, the Chinese Premier dismissed it off as beginner's luck.

A dwarf-alien carrying the container collapsed. Its partner, who ran to its rescue, slumped. A few more coming out of Saubha fell. One after another, the dwarf-aliens passed out with some of them crushed under their containers. It was as if someone aimed at them with great precision and shot them down. Like the sinking of the Titanic, Saubha came crumbling down. The visible half crashed and caved into the ground. Clouds of dust and smoke rose. Pieces of debris were flying everywhere. The Chinese Premier was flummoxed and excited.

When the experts and military went looking at the crash site, the bodies of the dwarf-aliens began disintegrating. The debris slowly started to disappear. They could not lay their hands on any of the bodies. The decomposing happened quick, and there was no stink. The bodies simply disappeared.

A cool, autumnal breeze swept over Wang who stood amidst the carnage. The team members were sprawled everywhere trying to make sense of the disappearance. Empty as it was, Wang took a deep breath. It was 6:30 PM. Faint evening light faded to darkness. Wang strode towards the captain and touched his arm. The captain turned around and saw no one. He panicked.

Drawing himself away from the noisy commotion, Wang left to trek the sacred Mount Kailash. None dared to set foot on it. Behind him, the chants were waning away. Wang had evolved. Completely invisible at will, it dawned on Wang that he was now more than a human being.

***

AUTHOR'S NOTE

Thank you so much for reading The Power of Zero and other sci-fi stories. This book allowed me to explore a new way of looking at science fiction through the ancient Vedic wisdom. I used to find science fiction too supernatural to my taste, sometimes bordering on the bizzare. But, with a firm footing in Indian Vedic 'mythology', my outlook to science fiction transformed completely. I hope to write more such stories for like-minded readers to enjoy.